Bad Bear

To Finbar, our very own Bad Bear

Other titles in this series include:

Daft Dog
Greedy Goat
Crazy Cow
Rude Rabbit
Happy Horse

First published in hardback in Great Britain by HarperCollins Publishers Ltd in 2001
First published in paperback by Collins Picture Books in 2002
1 3 5 7 9 10 8 6 4 2
ISBN: 0-00-664719-7

Copyright © Colin and Jacqui Hawkins 2001
The authors assert the moral right to be identified as the authors of the work.

Printed and bound in Singapore by Imago

Bad Bear

Colin and Jacqui Hawkins

Collins

An imprint of HarperCollins*Publishers*

This is Bad Bear.

Bad Bear loved going to the cinema. He liked adventure films the best, especially starring his hero, Desperate Dog. "Wow!" thought Bad Bear as he watched Desperate Dog's latest film. "I want to be a baddie like that," and he galloped off home.

Bad Bear put on his Desperate Dog outfit, and filled up his water pistol.
"Yahoo! I'm a rootin', tootin', galamalootin', water shootin' Bad Bear!" he yelled and set off.
On the way into town he took Mrs Cow's washing line from her garden.
"Yahoo!" he said. "I need a lasso!" And he ran off whirling the rope around his head.
"Mooo! Mooo!" bellowed Mrs Cow. "How dare yooooooou!"

In town Bad Bear was very bad… He squirted water at Daft Dog. He grabbed a fat fish from Mr Flipper's fish shop and popped Mr Flipper on the nose with his pop gun.

"Oww! You bad bear!" honked Mr Flipper.
"That's nnnot fffunny!"
Next Bad Bear swiped some sticky cakes from
Mr Bun the baker.
"You're a bad bear!" trumpeted Mr Bun.
"Yup! I sure am!" laughed Bad Bear.

Outside the supermarket Bad Bear lassoed Mrs Sheep's shopping trolley.

"Yee-hah! Wagons roll!" shouted Bad Bear.

"You baaad, baaad, bear!" bleated Mrs Sheep.

"Baaad, baaad bear!" bleated all the little sheep.
"Yup! I'm the baaaaaadest bear in town!"
laughed Bad Bear and he ran off.

Bad Bear's badness became unbearable.

He even lassoed Rude Rabbit and tied him to a lamppost.

This made Rude Rabbit very rude indeed.

"You're a BAD, BAD, BAD, BAD BEAR!" shouted Rude Rabbit.

"Yup! Yes sirree! I sure am!" giggled Bad Bear as he galloped away.

Bad Bear went from bad to worse and everyone got very fed up.

"We must doooo something about Bad Bear," bellowed Mr Cow.

Soon big posters appeared in every shop all over town saying:

BEWARE BAD BEAR!
BAD BEAR IS BAD!
BAD BEAR IS BANNED!

"Aw! Shucks!" said Bad Bear. "I'm a banned bear. There's no place for me to go… except…

the cinema!"
Bad Bear had a
wonderful time
watching the latest
film. "Wow!" he
said. "That was
super!"

Bad Bear rushed
home and
rummaged in
his wardrobe.

He found some
tights, took down
some curtains,

painted an old pair of boots,
cut up some cloth and
sewed it together.

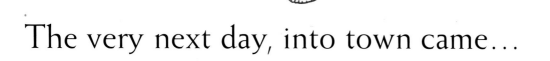

The very next day, into town came…

Bat Bear was a super hero. He rescued Kitty Kitten from a high tree, he saved Greedy Goat after she had chewed a big hole in her boat, he carried Mrs Sheep's shopping, and he helped the little sheep across the road.

One day Bat Bear was in the park when he heard Mrs Pig squeal, "Help! Help! My babies!" The little pigs were hurtling down the hill towards the pond! With super speed, Bat Bear leapt into action. In the nick of time, he grabbed the pram and saved the little pigs. "Thank you! Thank you, Bat Bear!" squeaked the little pigs. "You saved our bacon!"

"Just doing my job, folks," grinned Bat Bear. And with a swirl of his cape he was gone…

After that, whenever daring deeds needed to be done, Bat Bear would appear and say,

   "NEVER FEAR, BAT BEAR IS HERE!"

And what happened to Bad Bear?
Well, he still *POPS* up from time to time!